Dear Parents:

Congratulations! Your child is taking the first steps on an exciting journey. The destination? Independent reading!

STEP INTO READING® will help your child get there. The program offers five steps to reading success. Each step includes fun stories and colorful art or photographs. In addition to original fiction and books with favorite characters, there are Step into Reading Non-Fiction Readers, Phonics Readers and Boxed Sets, Sticker Readers, and Comic Readers—a complete literacy program with something to interest every child.

Learning to Read, Step by Step!

Ready to Read   Preschool–Kindergarten
• big type and easy words • rhyme and rhythm • picture clues
For children who know the alphabet and are eager to begin reading.

Reading with Help   Preschool–Grade 1
• basic vocabulary • short sentences • simple stories
For children who recognize familiar words and sound out new words with help.

Reading on Your Own   Grades 1–3
• engaging characters • easy-to-follow plots • popular topics
For children who are ready to read on their own.

Reading Paragraphs   Grades 2–3
• challenging vocabulary • short paragraphs • exciting stories
For newly independent readers who read simple sentences with confidence.

Ready for Chapters   Grades 2–4
• chapters • longer paragraphs • full-color art
For children who want to take the plunge into chapter books but still like colorful pictures.

STEP INTO READING® is designed to give every child a successful reading experience. The grade levels are only guides; children will progress through the steps at their own speed, developing confidence in their reading.

Remember, a lifetime love of reading starts with a single step!

Step into Reading, Random House, and the Random House colophon are registered trademarks of Penguin Random House LLC.

Visit us on the Web!
rhcbooks.com

Educators and librarians, for a variety of teaching tools, visit us at RHTeachersLibrarians.com

ISBN 978-0-7364-4489-7 (trade) — ISBN 978-0-7364-9050-4 (lib. bdg.)
ISBN 978-0-7364-4490-3 (ebook)

Printed in the United States of America

10 9 8 7 6 5 4 3 2 1

Disney

MOANA 2

Moana's Canoe Crew

adapted by Natasha Bouchard

illustrated by the Disney Storybook Art Team

Random House 🏠 New York

Moana sails across the ocean, hoping to meet people from distant shores.

Moana must travel
to a lost island and
reunite all the people
of the ocean.

Moana's journey will
be long and dangerous.
She gathers a crew
to help her.

Loto builds canoes.
Her repairing skills
will come in handy.

Kele is the island's best farmer. He will make sure there is food to eat.

Moni is a storyteller.
He knows the history
of the ocean and the
islands.

Heihei and Pua are
Moana's loyal friends.
They are always
ready to help.

Heihei is not scared
of anything.
Pua tries to be brave
for Moana.

Moana and her crew
sail off to search
for the lost island,
called Motufetū.

The crew has never
gone on a big voyage.
They have a lot to
learn about sailing!

Moni watches Moana
feel the current to
make sure they are
going the right way.

The crew learns how
to steer the canoe
and measure the stars.

Moana shows Loto
how to raise the sail.
This will help the
canoe go faster.

Oh no! The Kakamora
have arrived!
They don't want to fight.
They tell the crew that
they are also searching
for Motufetū.

Kotu is the son of
the Kakamora chief.
Kotu will join
Moana's crew.

But Moana's crew is not complete without Maui. His hook gives him magical powers!

Maui uses his special
powers to help the
crew reach Motufetū.

Moana can sail through any problem with the help of her canoe crew!